'Twas the Night Before Christmas

Clement C. Moore

Illustrated by Deborah Melmon

Highlights Press
Honesdale, Pennsylvania

'Twas the Night Before Christmas
when all through the house,

not a creature was stirring,

not even a mouse.

The stockings were hung

by the chimney with care

in hopes that St. Nicholas

soon would be there.

We children were nestled
all snug in our beds,

while visions of sugar-plums
danced in our heads.
And Mama in her 'kerchief
and Pa in his cap,
had just settled down
for a long winter's nap.

4

When out on the lawn
there arose such a clatter,

we sprang from the bed

to see what was the matter.

Away to the window

we flew like a flash,

tore open the shutters

and threw up the sash.

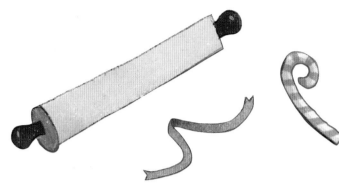

The moon on the crest
of the new-fallen snow

gave the luster of midday

to objects below.

When what to our wondering eyes

should appear,

but a miniature sleigh

and eight tiny reindeer.

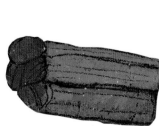

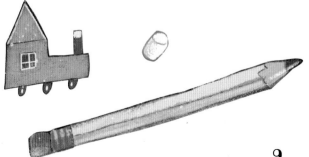

With a little old driver,
so lively and quick,

we knew in a moment
it must be St. Nick.
More rapid than eagles
his reindeer they came,
and he whistled, and shouted,
and called them by name.

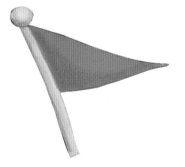

"Now, Dasher! Now, Dancer!
Now, Prancer and Vixen!

On, Comet! On, Cupid!

On, Donner and Blitzen!

To the top of the porch!

To the top of the wall!

Now dash away! Dash away!

Dash away all!"

As dry leaves that before
the wild hurricane fly

when they meet with an obstacle,

mount to the sky;

so up to the housetop

the reindeer they flew,

with the sleigh full of toys

and St. Nicholas too.

And then, in a twinkling,
we heard on the roof,

the prancing and pawing of

each little hoof.

As we drew in our heads and

were turning around,

down the chimney St. Nicholas

came with a bound.

He was dressed all in fur,
from his head to his foot,

and his clothes were all tarnished

with ashes and soot.

A bundle of toys

he had flung on his back,

and he looked like a peddler

just opening his pack.

19

His eyes—how they twinkled!
His dimples—how merry!

His cheeks were like roses,
his nose like a cherry!
His droll little mouth
was drawn up like a bow,
and the beard of his chin
was as white as the snow.

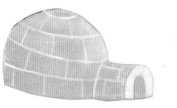

He had a broad face
and a little round belly,
that shook when he laughed,

like a bowlful of jelly.

He was chubby and plump,

a right jolly old elf,

and we laughed when we saw him,

in spite of ourselves.

A wink of his eye and a

twist of his head

soon gave us to know

we had nothing to dread.

23

MOM DAD MAX CJ AVA FLUFFY

Santa

24

He spoke not a word,
but went straight to his work,

and filled all the stockings,

then turned with a jerk.

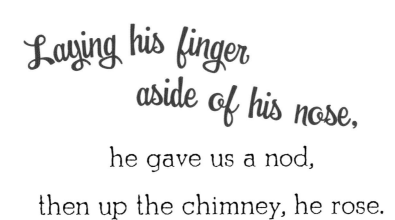

Laying his finger
aside of his nose,

he gave us a nod,

then up the chimney, he rose.

He sprang to his sleigh,

to his team gave a whistle,

and away they all flew

like the down of a thistle.

But we heard him exclaim,

as he drove out of sight,

"Merry Christmas to all,
and to all a good night!"

Dear Reader,

Every illustration in this book is also a Hidden Pictures puzzle. The picture clues around the text on each page can help you find the objects hidden in the illustration. If you are having trouble finding an object, here are a few tips:

- Look for objects that may be hidden in plain sight, disguised to look like something else.
- Try turning the book on its side to study the picture from a different angle.
- Try looking in an area where you haven't found anything yet.

Page 1

Can You Find:

- skateboard
- bicycle
- slipper
- car
- fork
- jack
- acorn
- feather
- winter hat
- ski
- pinecone
- sock

Pages 2-3

Can You Find:

- top hat
- scarf
- baseball
- toothbrush
- waterbottle
- drum
- owl
- star
- snowball
- sunglasses
- pinecone
- button

Pages 4-5

Can You Find:

- birdcage
- scarf
- ski pole
- dog bone
- feather
- musical note
- cupcake
- button
- magnifying glass
- ice skate
- sunglasses
- sailboat

Pages 6-7

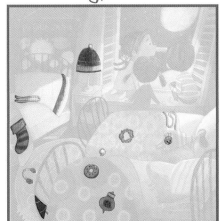

Can You Find:

- winter hat
- ski
- train track
- stocking
- piece of popcorn
- wreath
- ribbon
- jingle bell
- earmuffs
- doughnut
- spinning top
- ornament

Pages 8-9

Can You Find:
- firewood
- pencil
- envelope
- winter hat
- train
- ribbon
- gift
- candy cane
- teapot
- angel
- rolling pin
- marshmallow

Pages 10-11

Can You Find:
- domino
- artist's brush
- clock
- hockey stick
- lollipop
- pennant
- holly leaf
- candy cane
- snow shovel
- key
- open book
- quilt

Pages 12-13

Can You Find:
- key
- candle
- horn
- drum
- mug
- magnet
- comb
- crown
- mitten
- domino
- ice skate
- ring

Pages 14-15

Can You Find:
- cookie
- crescent moon
- mistletoe
- icicle
- horn
- open book
- holly leaf
- cupcake
- train
- ladder
- crown
- piece of popcorn

Pages 16-17

Can You Find:
- puzzle piece
- loaf of bread
- camera
- fairy
- ball
- carrot
- winter hat
- sleigh
- needle
- Christmas card
- teapot
- belt

Pages 18-19

Can You Find:
- magnet
- spoon
- stocking
- angel
- snowflake
- skateboard
- lollipop
- pennant
- twine
- heart
- bowl
- scissors

Pages 20-21

Can You Find:

- cardinal
- crown
- cherry
- swan
- crescent moon
- snowball
- crayon
- rabbit
- feather
- reindeer
- igloo
- snow angel

Pages 22-23

Can You Find:

- ring
- penguin
- crescent moon
- domino
- cloud
- jingle bell
- ruler
- golf club
- holly leaf
- pear
- leaf
- paintbrush

Pages 24-25

Can You Find:

- key
- puzzle piece
- mug
- ribbon
- comb
- feather
- pinecone
- orange
- top hat
- two gold rings
- magnifying glass
- partridge

Pages 26-27

Can You Find:

- fruitcake
- candy
- snowman
- game piece
- ladle
- wristwatch
- drumstick
- candle
- pretzel
- teacup
- bell
- envelope

Pages 28-29

Can You Find:

- scissors
- musical note
- crayon
- ice skate
- pinecone
- present
- mug
- harp
- sailboat
- key
- acorn
- North Pole

For information about permission to reprint selections from this book, please contact permissions@highlights.com.

Published by Highlights Press
815 Church Street
Honesdale, Pennsylvania 18431
Manufactured in Heshan, Guangdong, China
ISBN: 978-1-68437-649-0
Library of Congress Control Number: 2018956743
Mfg. 07/2021

First edition
Visit our website at Highlights.com.
10 9 8 7 6 5 4